Twenty Jātaka Tales

Twenty Jātaka Tales

Retold by *Noor Inayat Khan*

Illustrated by *H. Willebeek Le Mair*

Inner Traditions International
Rochester, Vermont

Inner Traditions International, Ltd.
One Park Street
Rochester, Vermont 05767

LIBRARY OF CONGRESS CATALOGING-IN-PUBLICATION DATA

Khan, Noor Inayat.
    Twenty Jātaka tales / retold by Noor Inayat Khan : illus-
trated by H. Willebeek Le Mair.
        p. cm.
    Summary: Recounts how Buddha came once as a monkey
among the monkeys and gave his life to save them, and nine-
teen other Jātaka stories which recount events in his different
lives.
    ISBN 0-89281-323-7
    1. Jātaka stories, English. [1. Jātaka stories.] I. Willebeek
le Mair, H. (Henriëtte), 1889–1966, ill. II. Title.
[BQ1462.E5K47 1991]
294.3'823—dc20   91–8318
                                                              CIP
Printed and bound in the United States

10   9   8   7   6   5   4   3   2   1

Distributed to the book trade in the United States by American
International Distribution Corporation (AIDC)

Distributed to book trade in Canada by Book Center, Inc.,
Montreal, Quebec

Text Design by Randi Jinkins

The author has drawn upon the following standard books in retelling these tales, and she gratefully acknowledges the permission given by their publishers: *The Gâtakamâlâ* or *Garland of Birth-stories* by Âyre Sûra, translated from the Sanskrit by J. S. Speyer (Oxford University Press), and *Jātaka* or *Stories of Buddha's Former Births,* translated from the Pali (Cambridge University Press).

Contents

Illustrations

And while the Buddha sat, and all around him listened, these are the stories he told.

"My children," he said, "I have not come now among you as your Buddha for the first time; I have come many times before; sometimes as a child among the little children, sometimes among the animals as one of their kind, loving them as I love you now; sometimes in Nature, among the flowers, I traced a way for you and you knew it not.

"Thus your Buddha came once as a monkey amid the monkeys, as a deer amid the deer, and he was their chief and their guide."

∼ 1 ∼

The Monkey-bridge

With a mighty effort he clung to the branch

giant-like monkey once ruled over eighty thousand monkeys in the Himalaya mountains. And through the rocks where they lived streamed the river Ganges before reaching the valley where cities were built. And there where the bubbling water fell from rock to rock stood a magnificent tree. In the spring it bore tender white blossoms; and later it was laden with fruit so wonderful that none could be compared to them, and the sweet winds of the mountain gave them the sweetness of honey.

How happy the monkeys were! They ate the fruit and lived in the shade of the wonderful tree. From one side of the tree the branches spread over the water. Therefore, when the blossom appeared the monkeys ate or destroyed the flowers on those branches that the fruit might not grown on them, and if a fruit did grow they plucked it, were it no larger than the heart of a blossom, for the chief, seeing the danger, had warned them, saying: "Beware, let not a fruit fall into the water lest the river carry it to the city, where men seeing the beautiful fruit might search for the tree; fol-

lowing the river up into the hills, and, finding
the tree, they would take all the fruit and we
should have to flee from here." Thus the monkeys obeyed and for a long time never a fruit
fell into the river. But the day came when one
ripe fruit hidden by an ant's nest, unseen between the leaves, fell into the water and was
taken by the flow of the river down, down the
rocky hills, into the valley where the large city
of Benares stands at the bank of the Ganges.
And that day, while the fruit passed by Benares,
pushed along by the little waves of the river,
the King Brahmadatta was bathing in the water
between two nets which some fishermen held
while he plunged and swam and played with
the little sunrays caught in the water. And the
fruit floated into one of the nets.

"Wonderful!" exclaimed the fisherman who
saw it first. "Where on this earth grows such
a fruit as this?" And, seizing it, with sparkling
eyes he showed it to the King.

Brahmadatta gazed at the fruit and marvelled
at its beauty. "Where is the tree which bears
this fruit to be found?" he wondered. Then,
calling some woodcutters from near the river-

bank, he asked if they knew of the fruit and where it could be found.

"Sire," they said, "it is a mango, a wonderful mango. Such a fruit as this grows not in our valley, but up in the hills of the Himalaya, where the air is pure and the sunrays undisturbed. No doubt the tree stands on the riverside and a fruit having fallen in the water has been carried here."

The King then asked the men to taste of it, and when they had done so, he also tasted it, and gave of it to his ministers and attendants. "Indeed," they said, "such a fruit is divine; never can another be compared to this."

The days and the nights went slowly by and Brahmadatta grew more and more restless. The longing to taste of the fruit once again became stronger as each day passed. In the night he saw in his dreams the enchanted tree carrying on each branch a hundred golden cups of honey and nectar.

"Indeed it must be found," said the King one day, and he gave orders that a boat be prepared to sail up the river Ganges, up to the Himalaya rocks where perhaps the tree might be found. And Brahmadatta went himself with the men.

Long indeed was the journey passing the fields of flowers and rice, but at last the King and his followers reached the Himalaya hills one evening, and gazing in the distance what did they see? There, beneath the moonlight, stood the longed-for tree, its golden fruit glittering through the leaves.

But what was moving on each branch? What strange little shadows were sliding through the leaves?

"See," said one of the men, "it is a troop of monkeys."

"Monkeys!" exclaimed the King; "eating the fruit! Surround the tree that they may not escape. At dawn we will shoot them and eat of their meat and of the mangoes."

These words came to the ears of the monkeys and, trembling, they said to their leader: "Alas! you warned us, beloved chief, but some fruit may have fallen in the stream, for men have come here; they surround our tree, and we cannot escape, for the distance between this tree and the next is too far for us to leap.

We heard words coming from the mouth of one of the men saying: 'At dawn we will shoot them and eat of their meat and of the mangoes.' "

"I will save you, my little ones," said the chief, "fear not, but do as I say." Thus consoling them, the mighty chief climbed to the highest branch of the tree. And as swift as wind passing through the rocks, he jumped a hundred bow lengths through space and landed on a tree near the opposite bank. There, at the edge of the water, he took a long reed from its very root and he thought: "I will bind one end of the reed to this tree and the other end to my foot. Then I will spring again to the mango tree; thus a bridge will be made over which my subjects may flee. A hundred bow lengths I have jumped. The reed is so much longer than a hundred bow lengths that I can bind one end to this tree." And his heart filled with joy he sprang back to the mango tree.

But, alas! the reed was too short and he was only just able to seize the end of a branch. It had not occurred to him that the reed should have been long enough to allow of the fastening to his foot. With a might effort he clung to the branch and called to his eighty thousand followers: "Run over my back on to the reed, and you will be saved."

One by one the monkeys ran over him on to the reed. But one among them called Devadatta jumped heavily upon his back. Alas! a piercing pain seized him; his back was broken. And the heartless Devadatta went on his way leaving his chief to suffer alone.

Brahmadatta had seen all that had happened and tears streamed from his eyes as he gazed upon the stricken monkey chief. He ordered that he be brought down from the tree to which he still clung, that he be bathed in the sweetest perfumes and clothed in a yellow garment, and that sweet water be given him to drink. And when the chief was bathed and clad, he lay beneath the tree and the King sat at his side and spoke to him. He said: "You made of your body a bridge for others to cross. Did you not know that your life would come to an end in so doing? You have given your life to save your followers. Who are you, blessed one, and who are they?"

"O King," replied the monkey, "I am their chief and their guide. They lived with me in this tree, and I was their father and I loved them. I do not suffer in leaving this world for I have gained my subjects' freedom. And if my death may be a lesson to you, then I am more than happy. It is not your sword which makes you a king; it is love alone. Forget not that your life is but little to give if in giving you secure the happiness of your people. Rule them not through power because they are your subjects; nay, rule them through love because they are your children. In this way only you shall be king. When I am no longer here forget not my words, O Brahmadatta!"

The Blessed One then closed his eyes and died.

But the King and his people mourned for him and the King built for him a temple pure and white that his words might never be forgotten.

And Brahmadatta ruled with love over his people and they were happy ever after.

2

The Guilty Dogs

Tell me, then, who are the guilty ones?

ne day, a king drove through the city in his magnificent chariot drawn by six white horses. And at the fall of night, when he returned, the horses were taken to the stable, but the chariot was left in the courtyard with the harnesses.

And when everyone was asleep in the palace, it started to rain.

"This is our time to have some fun," said the palace dogs, when they saw the leather harnesses wet and softened by the shower. Down they went, on tip-toe, into the courtyard, and bit and gnawed at the beautiful straps. And after thus playing the whole night, they slipped away before the dawn.

"The straps of the royal chariot, eaten! . . . destroyed! . . ." exclaimed with horror the stablemen as they entered the courtyard the next morning. And with trembling hearts they went to tell the King.

"Gracious lord," they said, "the trappings of the royal chariot have been destroyed during the night. It is certainly the work of dogs, who have been gnawing the beautiful straps."

The King rose up in fury.

"Kill them all," he commanded. "Slay every dog you see in the city."

The King's order soon became known to the seven hundred dogs of the city and they all cried bitterly. But there was one dog who was their chief, for he loved them and protected them, and in a long procession they set out to find him.

"Why are you gathered together today?" asked the chief, as he saw them come, "and what makes you all so sad?"

"Danger is upon us," replied the dogs; "the leather of the royal chariot, which stood during the night in the palace courtyard, has been destroyed, and we are blamed for the damage. The King is furious and has ordered us all to be killed."

"It is impossible for any dog of the city to enter the palace gates," thought the chief. "Who therefore could have destroyed the harnesses if not the dogs of the palace? Thus the guilty ones are spared and the innocent ones are to be destroyed. Nay, I will show the guilty ones to the King, and the city dogs shall be saved."

Such were the thoughts of the brave chief, and after consoling his seven hundred followers, he went alone through the city. At every step men were standing ready to kill him, but his eyes were so full of love that they did not dare touch him. And he walked into the palace, and the royal guards, spellbound at his appearance, let him pass through the gates.

Thus he entered into the hall of justice where the King sat on his throne and the courtiers stood around; and at sight of his fiery eyes, all remained silent.

After some time the chief spoke.

"Great King," he said, "is it your command that all the dogs of the city be killed?"

"Yes," replied the King, "it is my command."

"What harm have they done, O King?" he asked.

"They have destroyed the leather harnesses of the royal chariot," the King replied.

"Which dogs have done the harm?" asked the chief.

"I know not," replied the King; "therefore have I ordered them all to be killed."

"Is every dog of your city to be killed," asked

the chief, "or are some dogs to be allowed to live?"

"The royal dogs only are to be allowed to live," the King replied.

"O King," said the chief in a gentle voice, "is your command just? Why should the dogs of the palace be innocent and the dogs of the city be judged guilty? The ones you favor are saved and the ones you know not are to be killed. O just King, where is your justice?"

The King thought for awhile and then said:

"Wise chief, tell me, then, who are the guilty ones?"

"The royal dogs," replied the chief.

"Show me that your words are true," said the King.

"I will show you," answered the chief. "Order that the palace dogs be brought here to the hall of justice and be given kusa grass and buttermilk to eat."

The King did as the chief asked, and the royal dogs were brought before him and given kusa grass and buttermilk to eat.

Soon after they had eaten, shreds of leather

came out of their mouths and fell on the ground. The guilty ones were found.

The King rose gently from his throne. "Your words are true," he said to the wise chief, "true and pure, as the raindrops which fall from the sky. I shall never forget you as long as I live."

He then ordered that all the dogs of the city be given rich food and royal care every day of their lives, and they all lived happy every after.

3

Banyan

"Return to your little one," said Banyan

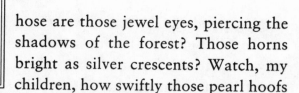

hose are those jewel eyes, piercing the shadows of the forest? Those horns bright as silver crescents? Watch, my children, how swiftly those pearl hoofs pass through the bushes! Have you not heard about the golden deer, my little ones? 'Banyan,' the King of the deer, he is called.

But Banyan was not the only monarch in the forest of Benares. He reigned over five hundred deer and another king, 'Branch,' ruled another five hundred.

It was the habit of the King of Benares to hunt the deer each day. Before reaching the forest there were numberless fields to cross, and the rice, the corn, and the tender plants which the peasants cultivated were trampled by the horses of the King and his noblemen. "Mercy," cried the peasants, but the trumpets blew and their poor voices were lost in the fields.

"How can we change this?" thought the peasants. "Let us chase all the deer into the King's own gardens, then he will no more pass through our fields to hunt."

Thus the peasants, after sowing grass and

digging ponds in the palace woods, called the men of the city, and with sticks and spears they went to the forest to chase the deer. The men first surrounded the forest, that from no side the deer might escape, and then clashing their spears and weapons they drove the deer into the woods of the palace and closed the gates behind them. Then they went to the King and said: "Sire, we could no longer work. Alas! when you and your noblemen went hunting our fields were trampled by the horses; therefore have we driven the deer into the palace woods; we have sown grass and dug ponds that they may eat and drink. Thus you need no longer cross our fields."

From that time the King went no farther than his woods to hunt. Each day he watched the beautiful herd, and he saw that among them were two golden ones. "The golden deer must not be killed," he said to his men; thus Banyan Deer and Branch Deer were never touched by the piercing arrows. But of the others one was killed each day for the feast of the King, after having been wounded over and over

again. And some deer were wounded a thousand times before at last they fell to the arrow
of the hunters.

Branch, therefore, went one day to Banyan,
and said: "Friend of the woods, take heed of
my words. Our subjects are not only being
killed but wounded uselessly. Alas! one must
be killed each day, such is the wish of the
King, but why should so many be wounded
before one alone is caught? Would it not be
wiser if each day one of our subjects went to
the palace to be killed?"

Banyan agreed, and so it was ordered. Each
day in turn a deer went to the palace and placed
its pure white forehead on the stone before the
door. One day one of Banyan's herd, and the
next day one of Branch's.

Now one day a young doe of the herd of
Branch, mother of a small baby-deer, was told
that her turn had come. Upon hearing the news
she ran to Branch and said: "Lord, this day
my turn has come to go to the palace, but my
little one is weak and still needs a mother's
care. May I not go later when he is older?"

"Go," said Branch; "another cannot take your turn; go to the palace as it has been ordered you to do."

Her little heart trembling with sorrow, the doe ran to Banyan and said: "O King Banyan, my turn has come to go to the palace, but I have a little one who needs me still. Can I not go a little later when he is older?"

"Return to your little one," said Banyan; "I will see that another takes your turn." And as lightning pierces the clouds, he ran through the trees and the bushes and bent his forehead to the stone before the palace door.

"O golden one! Here on this stone to be killed! Oh, what does it mean?" exclaimed the man who each day killed a deer for the feast of the King. His knife fell to the ground, and, spellbound, he ran to the King to tell him what he had seen. Just as you, my little one, would run to the brother who is dear to you, thus the King ran to Banyan. "O beautiful one," he exclaimed, "what has brought you to this stone of pain? Did you not know I ordered that you must never be killed? Golden deer, tell me what has brought you here?"

"Lord," replied Banyan, "today was the turn of a white doe, mother of a small deer; I came in her place, for her little one is yet too young to be alone."

Tears streamed down the cheeks of the King and fell on the golden head of Banyan, which he held between his hands. And bending over Banyan, he said: "Your life, O divine one, and the life of the doe shall be spared. Arise, and run into the woods again."

"Lord," answered Banyan, "our lives are to be spared, but what of our kindred who run within the woods?"

"Their lives shall also be spared," replied the King.

"Thus the deer in the woods of the palace are saved, but what of all the other deer in your kingdom, Lord?"

"They, too, shall all be spared," answered the King.

"O King," said Banyan, "you will spare the deer, but what of the lives of all other four-footed creatures?"

"O merciful one," said the King, "they shall all be free."

"Lord, they shall all be free, but what of the birds that fly through space?"

"They shall be spared also," said the King.

"Lord," said Banyan, "you will spare the lives of the four-footed creatures and of the birds, but what of the fish that live in the water?"

"They shall be spared also," said the King.

Love had entered into the heart of the King. And he reigned with love over his people, and all the living creatures in his realm were happy ever after.

4

The Tortoise
and the Geese

Off they flew over the mountaintops, and the whole world lay beneath them

"ome with us, friend Tortoise," said one day two wild geese to a kind old tortoise who lived in a pond in the Himalayas. "We have a fine home in a golden cave on the mount Cittakutta."

"I have no wings," replied the tortoise. "How can I reach your home?"

"Can you keep your mouth closed?" asked the geese.

"Yes, certainly," he replied.

"Hold then this stick between your teeth," said the geese, "and we will take each end within our beaks and carry you through the air."

And off they flew over the mountain-tops, and the whole world lay beneath them. But after some time they flew over the roofs of Benares.

"How strange!" laughed some children who saw them pass. "A tortoise is being carried by geese through the air!"

Master Tortoise, hearing these words, became very restless and a tiny anger-fire began to blaze in his small heart.

"Why should you care if I am carried

through the sky?" he cried aloud. Of course he could not speak without opening his mouth; his teeth lost their hold of the stick, and down fell poor Master Tortoise into the courtyard of the palace of the King. In a moment, the Court was aroused. Ministers, noblemen, and royal guards stood at every window and every door. News was brought to the King, who rose from his throne and went to the scene together with his counselor, a wise man of the Court.

"Poor tortoise!" exclaimed the King. "What caused him to fall in this courtyard, and break his beautiful green shell?"

"Tell me," he said to his counselor, "from where has he fallen and why did he fall?"

Now, my children, it so happened that the King's habit was to talk very much. He was kind and good-hearted, but in his presence it was difficult for others to get in a word. Thus the counselor, knowing the reason of the tortoise's fall, thought: "Here is my chance to give our talkative King a lesson."

"Lord," he said, "some birds were carrying a tortoise through the air by holding between them in their beaks a stick, to which he clung with his teeth. The tortoise heard the children in the city laughing at him. This no doubt made him angry and he could not forbear speaking to them, wherefore he lost hold of the stick and fell. Such is the fate that comes to those who cannot hold their tongues."

These words pierced the King's heart; he knew that the lesson was meant for him, and from that day his words were few and wise; he talked only when it was time to speak, and he lived happy ever after.

5

The Fairy
and the Hare

Full of joy the hare jumped into the glowing fire

 young hare once lived in a small forest between a mountain, a village, and a river. My children, many hares run through the heather and the moss, but none as sweet as he.

Three friends he had: a jackal, a water-weasel, and a monkey.

After the long day's toil, searching for food, they came together at evening, all four, to talk and think. The handsome hare spoke to his three companions and taught them many things. And they listened to him and learned to love all the creatures of the woods, and they were very happy.

"My friends," said the hare one day, "let us not eat tomorrow, but the food we find in the day we will give to any poor creature we meet."

This they all agreed to. And the next day, as every day, they started out at dawn in search of food.

The jackal found in a hut in the village a piece of meat and a jar of curdled milk with a rope tied to each handle. Three times he cried aloud: "Whose is this meat? Whose is this curdled milk?" But the hut was empty, and hearing no answer, he put the piece of meat in his mouth, and the rope of the jar around his neck, and away he fled to the forest. And laying them at his side he thought: "What a good jackal I am! Tomorrow I shall eat what I have found if no one comes this way."

And what did little water-weasel find on his rounds?

A fisherman had caught some sparkling golden fish, and after hiding them under the sand he returned to the river to catch more!

But the water-weasel found the hiding place, and after taking the fish out of the sand, he called three times: "Whose are these golden fish?"

But the fisherman heard only the rippling of the river and none answered his call! So he took the fish into the forest to his little home, and thought: "What a good water-weasel I am! These fish I shall not eat today, but perhaps another day."

Meanwhile monkey-friend had climbed the mountain, and finding some ripe mangoes, he carried them down into the woods and put them under a tree, and he thought: "What a good monkey I am!"

But the hare lay in the grass in the woods, and his beautiful eyes were moist with sadness. "What can I offer if any poor creature should pass by the way?" he thought. "I cannot offer grass, and I have neither rice nor nuts to give."

But suddenly he leaped with joy. "If someone comes this way," he thought, "I shall give him myself to eat."

Now, in the sweet little wood lived a fairy with butterfly-wings, and long hair of moonlight-rays. Her name was Sakka. She knew everything that took place in the wood. She knew if a small ant had stolen from another ant. She knew the thoughts of all the little creatures, even of the poor little flowers, trampled over in the grass. And she knew that day that the four friends in the wood were not eating, and that any food that they might find was to be given to any poor creature they might meet.

And so Sakka changed herself into an old beggar man, bent over, walking with a stick.

She went first to the jackal and said: "I have walked for days and weeks, and have had nothing to eat. I have no strength to search for food! Pray give me something, O jackal!"

"Take this piece of meat, and this jar of curdled milk," said the jackal. "I stole it from a hut in the village, but it is all I have to give."

"I will see about it later," said the beggar, and she went on through the shady trees.

Then Sakka met the water-weasel and asked: "What have you to give to me, little one?"

"Take these fish, O beggar, and rest awhile beneath this tree," answered the water-weasel.

"Another time," the beggar replied, and passed on through the woods.

A little farther Sakka met the monkey and said: "Give me of your fruits, I pray. I am poor and starved and weary."

"Take all these mangoes," said the monkey. "I have plucked them all for you."

"Some other time," replied the beggar, and did not stay.

Then Sakka met the hare and said: "Sweet one of the mossy woods, tell me, where can I find food? I am lost within the forest and far away from home."

"I will give you myself to eat," replied the hare. "Gather some wood and make a fire; I will jump into the flames and you shall then have the flesh of a little hare."

Sakka caused magic flames to rise from some logs of wood, and full of joy the hare jumped into the glowing fire. But the flames were cool as water, and did not burn his skin.

"Why is it," said he to Sakka, "I do not feel the flames? The sparks are as fresh as the dew of the dawn."

Sakka then changed herself into her fairy form again, and spoke to the hare in a voice sweeter than any voice he had ever heard.

"Dear one," she said, "I am the fairy Sakka. This fire is not real, it is only a test. The kindness of your heart, O blessed one, shall be known throughout the world for ages to come."

So saying Sakka struck the mountain with her wand, and with the essence which gushed forth she drew the picture of the hare on the orb of the moon.

Next day the hare met his friends again, and all the creatures of the woods gathered round them. And the hare told them of all that had happened to him, and they rejoiced. And all lived happy ever after.

6

The Golden Feathers

The goose returned and gave them another feather

father and mother and their three daughters once lived in a small hut in the forest, for they were very poor. And one day the father said to his wife and daughters: "Good wife, and good little daughters, I must leave you for some time. But I shall return with many riches and beautiful things. My little daughters shall have many jewels to put in their hair; and you will all be happy."

After saying these words, the man set out on his long journey.

On his way he walked through the forest in the night, and a fairy met him. "Where are you going, O traveler, at this time of night?" she asked. "I am going to seek fortune," he replied. Without more words the fairy raised her wand and touched his shoulder, and he was changed into a goose with golden feathers.

The poor father, now changed into a goose, flew onto the branch of a tree and he thought: "What can I now do for my family? I am but a goose, I cannot seek for riches, and my wife and daughters are very poor." Such were his thoughts as he perched on the branch of the tree, and he was very, very sad. But suddenly he looked down and saw himself reflected in a pool of water beneath. "My feathers are gold!" he cried, shaking his wings with glee. And away he flew, to the little hut where his wife and daughters were waiting.

"Mother, a golden goose is coming to us!" exclaimed the daughters.

Alighting at the door the goose spoke to them. "Good people," he said, "I know you are poor, but, see, my feathers are of gold." And taking a feather from his back he gave it to them, saying: "Take then this one and sell it. I will return again by and by." And with that he flew back to the forest.

The wife sold the feather and received much money for it. And each time this was spent the goose returned and gave them another feather.

But one day the mother said to her daughters: "My children, this goose may one day fly away and never return. Next time he comes we must pluck off all his feathers."

The daughters wept bitterly at the thought of this ingratitude. But nevertheless when the goose returned their mother seized him and plucked all his feathers. Robbed of his plumage the goose was unable to fly, and his selfish wife threw him in a barrel and gave him but little food to eat.

But the feathers she plucked became white as the feathers of every other goose, for the fairy had given them a charm, a charm that would turn them white if ever they were taken from him.

After he had lived some time thus miserably in the barrel white feathers grew on the goose's wings again. He then flew away, far away to a forest where every bird was happy, and he lived happy with them ever after.

7

The Young Parrot

The young parrot brings food to his parents

At the top of a hill there was a wood of silk cotton trees, and in that wood lived a flock of parrots with their king and queen.

And the king and queen had a beautiful child-parrot, more beautiful than any parrot in the world!

Time passed and King and Queen Parrot grew old, and little child-parrot grew up to be all glorious and larger than any parrot in the world.

And he said one day to his parents: "Dear ones, now that I am grown and strong I will go to bring food from the fields for you."

And each day he flew with the flock to the rice fields. And after eating with the rest he took away in his beak a large share to give to his mother and father.

But one day the parrots found a beautiful field, more fertile than any other. And after that they went there to eat.

"I must tell my master that parrots are eating his rice," thought the farmer's man.

And he went to the farmer and said: "Master, our field is fertile and truly the rice is more beautiful than in any other field. But a flock of parrots come each day to feed of the grains, and one among them, more beautiful than the others, after eating a large share, leaves with a beak full of rice to store away."

The owner of the field thereupon was seized with longing to see this bird that took the rice away.

"Make a trap of horse-hair and catch that parrot," he said to his man, "but bring him to me alive."

The next day, the laborer set a trap, and, while landing, the young parrot felt his tiny foot caught. He did not cry or call for help, for he thought: "If my comrades know I am caught, they will be frightened and will not eat. I must wait till they have eaten, and then I will call."

And when they had eaten he called, but none came to help him; all, in fear, flew away.

He was left alone, and he cried bitterly.

"What have I done?" he thought. "Why do they leave me?"

Before long the laborer came to the trap, and, joyfully seizing the bird, he exclaimed:

"Why, you are the very one I wished to catch." And he brought him to his master. The field-owner took the parrot gently between his hands.

"My bird," he said, "have you a little farm somewhere? Is it there you hide away the rice? When you have eaten from my field, away you fly, your beak filled with grain, you naughty little bird!"

The parrot replied in a sweet human voice:

"A duty I fulfill each day,
A treasure do I store away."

"Tell me," said the field-owner, "what is the duty you fulfill, and the treasure which you store away?"

"My duty," said the parrot, "is to bring food to my parents who are old and cannot fly; and my treasure is a forest of love. In that forest, those who are weak are helped by stronger ones, and those who hunger are given food."

On hearing this the old man smiled. "The field belongs to you all," he said. "Fly back to your parents who are awaiting you. But return to my field each day."

The beautiful bird quickly flew back to the woods where his parents were calling for him. And all the other parrots gathered round and listened to the young parrot's story. All the parrots of the woods were united, and they lived happy ever after.

8

The Empty Lake

*Once upon a time in this lake of ours was a king,
a great king*

*I*n a beautiful lake, a lake covered with waterlilies, many fish had met together; they had gathered to hear a story told by one of them.

"Once upon a time," the story ran, "in this lake of ours was a king, a great king. He was a fish as we, with a golden back, but so much more golden still. Yes, those who live on earth have many stars in their sky at night, but he was the star of *our* sky, and when all was dark he lighted the way through the waters.

"Now it happened that Queen Rain forgot to send showers on earth before the time of heat. Day after day Mother Earth and the thirsty sunrays drank the water of our lake. And King Wind, blowing fire from east to west, took all but the last drops away. Alas! our lake became a pool, and each day crows came and devoured our companions.

"But our King, our dear King, spoke in a soft whisper, and his words reached far above the earth. Queen Rain, hearing his call, looked down from above, the fairies who carry the water vessels and those who lead the clouds through the sky awoke from their sleep, and

King Thunder, hearing the prayer, stood up and called to his army: 'I command you all: fire!'

"Immediately the whole world shook. The cloud-leaders marched through the sky; the cannons of King Thunder shot flashes of lightning from east to west; the great sky opened, showing the light within, and water poured forth.

"The raindrops fell heavily, but the sound was sweet to our ears, telling us what the fairies were saying in the sky. And as we listened, our little drooping heads were lifted again.

"But our King feared that the water vessels would be taken away before the lake was full, and he spoke louder:

'King of Thunder, Queen of Rain,
Show your power once again,
Pour the water more and more,
Till our lake is as before.'

"At these words the water rushed from the sky as from a mountain torrent. Thunder crashed and the whole world shook. The burning sunrays at last were covered and the crows chased far away.

"And descending slowly from the sky, King Thunder and Queen Rain flew from their abode, and came down on earth.

" 'It is your love, O sweet one,' they said to our King, 'which has caused the world to shake and streams of water to pour forth. Do not fear, dear one; never shall this lake be empty again, for your voice shall never be forgotten.'

"And the lake was filled, and the waterlilies grew again, and we have all lived happy ever after."

9

The Swan Kingdom

Sumukha alone remained with his lord

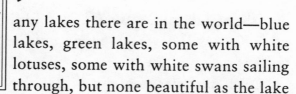

Many lakes there are in the world—blue lakes, green lakes, some with white lotuses, some with white swans sailing through, but none beautiful as the lake Manasa, for its water shone with all the colors of the sky. Miraculous flowers with large red cups of honey grew around its margins, and each day they dropped a little of their beauty in the lake.

In this kingdom lived sixty thousand swans, governed by King Dhritarashtra and Sumukha, the commander of his army.

The swans were beautiful as mermaids, and their army chief majestic and strong, but none could be compared to the King, for his feathers were of shining silver, and as he floated along in the night it was as if the moon were on the lake.

The courtiers in every palace spoke to their lords of this kingdom of swans. Many monarchs praised the wonderful nation and marvelled at their governors Dhritarashtra and Sumukha. But above all Brahmadatta, the King of Benares, thirsted to see them.

So it was that one day he gathered his

courtiers and said: "Wise and faithful ones, your King will never be happy until a certain wish is accomplished."

"Lord, may we know thy wish?" they asked.

"I long to meet the King and the commander of the lake Manasa; tell me, therefore, how may this wish be gratified?" replied the King.

"O King," said one of the courtiers, "if I may advise, there is only one way! At your order, a lake could be made near the gates of Benares even more splendid than the lake Manasa. And each day these words should be cried aloud: 'The King of Benares gives this lake to all the birds in the world, and they are protected by him.'

"The news would soon spread till the swans of lake Manasa, hearing that a more beautiful lake than theirs existed in the world, would hasten to see it."

This counsel was pleasing to the King and he gave orders that the work should begin. Trees with endless blossom and flowers from distant lands were brought. The lake was filled with water so clear that the fish could be seen swimming within. When the lake was finished it was grander by far than Manasa. And the birds, and the bees, and the butterflies came by thousands to sing and dance around.

Each day the call was heard, inviting the birds of other lands, and, coming from each quarter of the earth, they made the lake a meeting place.

One day two young swans of the lake Manasa left their kingdom to travel through the world. Passing over Benares they saw the enchanting lake and, hearing the call of invitation, they descended and gazed around them. A vision of beauty met their eyes. Such trees and flowers they had not even dreamed of; even garlands of flowers were floating gently upon the bosom of the lake.

"If only this was our kingdom!" they exclaimed. They sailed from one end of the lake to the other and then they lifted their wings and flew back to their home.

Day after day they spoke of the wonderful lake at the gates of Benares, and the sixty thousands swans became restless.

"Take us there, O King!" they asked Dhritarashtra each day, till at last he decided to leave. But Sumukha, the thoughtful one, did not rejoice. "My king," he said to Dhritarashtra, "are you quite sure that it is wise to please your subjects in this matter? Beware of the words of men; sweet indeed is the call of invitation, but we know little of what lies behind it. If, however, you have decided that we shall go, let us not stay longer than a day."

To this Dhritarashtra agreed, and at the fall of night the host of swans raised their wings and flew away to Benares. They reached the lake at dawn, and in a moment Manasa was forgotten and they swam through the flowers as if in a dream. They floated majestically upon the placid water, shining as sixty thousand stars from the sky, and word was brought to Brahmadatta, who cried aloud with joy: "Catch Dhritarashtra and Sumukha, and bring them to my palace."

The King's servants were not slow in setting a trap amid the flowers, and soon Dhritarashtra's silver foot was caught in it. Deeply alarmed, the sixty thousand swans arose with loud cries of pain and grief and flew wildly into the air, frantic as though their chief had been killed in battle. Sumukha alone remained with his lord.

"Return to Manasa," said Dhritarashtra to Sumukha; "my subjects cannot be happy alone. Go for their sake, O Sumukha! They need their chief to protect them on the lake."

But Sumukha would not hearken, and he stayed at his King's side.

When Brahmadatta's servant saw that one swan was caught, and that another stood waiting at his side, he gazed at them amazed.

"Your companion is caught," he said to Sumukha, "but you, O handsome one, are free. Why then do you stay? Do you not know that the guards can seize you? Your wings are white and fair; fly then away, brave one, and do not linger here."

But Sumukha answered in a human voice: "This bird you have caught is our king. How then can I flee from here and be happy far away from him? If you wish to please me, O guard, take me with you and set him free."

"Do not fear," replied the guard gently, "no harm will come to your king. True, his silver foot is caught, but only because our king Brahmadatta desires to see him. Come therefore on my shoulder to the palace. Our king will honor you both."

It was as the man had said, and when he had brought the swans unbound to the palace of the King, and had told Brahmadatta his story, the King stood speechless with awe and amazement. But Dhritarashtra spoke to him in a sweet voice and the heart of the King was drawn to him. They discoursed happily together, and after every royal favor had been shown to them the two swans departed from the Court and returned to Manasa.

It was a joyful homecoming for all sixty thousand swans and they lived together happy ever after.

~~10~~

The Master's Test

There is no place wherein no one is watching

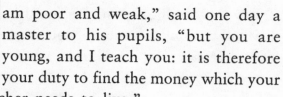

"I am poor and weak," said one day a master to his pupils, "but you are young, and I teach you: it is therefore your duty to find the money which your old teacher needs to live."

"How can we do so?" asked the pupils. "The people of this town are so little generous that it would be vain to ask them for help."

"My sons," replied the teacher, "there is a way to gain money, not by asking, but by taking. It would be no sin for us to steal, for we deserve money more than others. But alas! I am too old and weak to do it."

"We are young," replied the pupils; "we can do it. There is nothing we would not do for you, dear master. Tell us only how to act and we will obey."

"Young men you are," said the master; "it would be nothing to you to seize a rich man's purse. This is the way to do it: choose a quiet spot where no one watches, then catch hold of a passer-by and take his money, but do not do him harm."

"Straightaway we go," said all the pupils except one, who had been silent, his eyes cast downward.

The teacher looked at this youth and said: "My other pupils are courageous and eager to help, but little do you mind your teacher's suffering."

"Forgive me, master," he replied, "the plan you have explained seems to me impossible; that is the reason of my silence."

"Why is it impossible?" asked the master.

"Because there is no place wherein no one is watching," replied the pupil; "even when I am quite alone, my self is watching. I would rather take a bowl and beg, than allow my self to see me stealing."

At these words the master's face lighted up with joy. He took the young pupil in his arms and embraced him.

"Happy am I," he said, "if among my pupils one has understood my words."

His other pupils, seeing that their master had meant to test them, bent their heads in shame.

And after that day, whenever an unworthy thought came to their minds, they remembered their companion's words: "My self is watching."

Thus they became great men, and they all lived happy ever after.

11

The Two Pigs

*What is the pool of water and what is the perfume that
never fades away?*

"Tic-a-tac, who is passing by the way?" thought two little pigs at the edge of the village road. It was a little old woman, as round as the willow which bends into the lake.

Tic-a-tac, crack, crack! creaked her stick as she walked along, and four small, frightened eyes peeped through the grass.

"Who are you, little ones?" cried the old woman. "Has your mother left you all alone? Come into my basket; I will take you to my little home near the gates of Benares and be your mother."

And she took the two little pigs and put them in her basket, which was filled with cotton she had brought from the cottonfields. Then along she went, *tic-a-tac, crack, crack,* until she reached her little home, where she took the pigs out of the basket and put them on her knees, and she laughed and she smiled and was as happy as could be. She called the elder one Mahatundila and the younger one Cullatundila.

And days and years passed by, and the little old woman fed the two pigs and loved them as her own children.

But one day a big feast was held in the village near by. And the men of the village drank the whole day till they became very drunk, and having eaten all the meat that was in the village, and being still unsatisfied, they wanted more. They went therefore to the little old woman and said: "Mother, here is money; give us your pigs in return."

"Nay," she replied, "I shall not give them to you. Does one give away one's children for money?"

"They are not children, Mother, they are pigs," said the men. "What will you do with them later? Give them to us now, Mother, and all these golden coins shall be yours."

But the little old woman only shook her cunning little head.

Then the men made her drink, and when she was drunk they said to her again: "Mother, take this money and give us the pigs."

"I cannot give you Mahatundila, but take Cullatundila," she said, and putting rice in the little bowl at the door she called: "Cullatundila, Cullatundila!"

And Mahatundila, hearing the call, thought:

"Mother has never called Cullatundila first; she always calls me first. What danger is upon us to-day?"

Meanwhile Cullatundila went to the old woman, but seeing the bowl at the door and so many men standing around with ropes in hand he turned back and went to Mahatundila, his heart trembling with fear.

"Brother," said Mahatundila, "why are you trembling so?"

"Mother has put our bowl at the door and men are standing there with ropes. I fear, brother, some danger is upon us."

Mahatundila's soft eyes rested tenderly upon his brother, and in a low, sweet voice he said: "Your head is drooping, brother. Grieve not. Know that for this day we have been reared and fed. Alas! it is our flesh that men want. Go, Tundila; answer Mother's call."

Then, moved by the tears in his brother's eyes, he spoke these words:

> "Bathe in the pool of water as on a bright feast-day,
> And you shall find a perfume that never fades away."

And as he spoke all the world changed. The little flowers in the grass opened their hearts to listen, the trees bent over, the wind became silent, and the birds tarried in their flight. The men and the old woman were no longer drunk and the ropes fell from their hands. The sweet voice penetrated into the city of Benares and was heard by thousands of citizens, rich and poor. All were moved to tears and with one mind they hastened in the direction from which the voice came till they reached the little house where, breaking down the fence, they crowded around.

But Cullatundila was perplexed. "Why does my brother speak these words? We never bathe in a pool of water, neither do we find perfume."

"Brother, tell me," he said, "what is the pool of water and what is the perfume that never fades away?"

Mahatundila answered, and the great crowd stood silent as he spoke: "The pool of water is love, and love is the fragrance that never fades away. Be not sad, brother, be not sad to leave this world. Many stay and are unhappy; many leave and joy is theirs."

The sweet voice reached even through the marble dome of the Palace and the King of Benares was moved to tears.

As for the crowd, the thousands of citizens waved their hands and uttered loud and joyful cries. They then brought Mahatundila and Cullatundila to the palace, where the King gave orders that the brothers should be bathed in the sweetest perfume and clad in silken garments. They were given jewels to hang around their necks and thenceforward, while the King lived, they dwelt with him in the palace, and all disputes were brought to Mahatundila, the blessed one, and settled by him.

At last, in fullness of years, the King died and Mahatundila and his brother left the city to dwell in the forest, to the great grief of the people of Benares, who wept as they departed.

But the reign of justice did not end in the land. The people continued to dwell together in amity, and all lived happy ever after.

12

The Patient Buffalo

The mischievous monkey took a stick and knocked the buffalo's ears with it

giant-like buffalo with mighty horns lay under a tree asleep.

Two mischievous eyes peeped through the branches, and a little monkey said:

"I know a good old buffalo, who's sleeping 'neath the tree,
But I am not afraid of him, nor's he afraid of me."

And he leaped from the branch on to the buffalo's back.

The buffalo opened his eyes, and seeing the monkey dancing on his hip, he closed them again, as if only a butterfly were on his back.

Then rascal monkey tried another trick. Jumping on the buffalo's head between his two large horns, he held the ends and swung, as on a tree. But Buffalo did not even wink.

"What can I do to make my good friend angry?" he thought. And while buffalo was eating in the field, he trampled on the grass wherever he wished to graze. And the buffalo merely walked away.

Another day the mischievous monkey took

a stick and knocked the buffalo's ears with it, then while he was taking a walk he sat on his back like a hero, holding the stick in his hand.

And to all of this the buffalo made never a murmur, though his horns were strong and mighty.

But one day, while the monkey sat on his back, a fairy appeared.

"A great being you are, O buffalo," she said; "but little do you know your strength. Your horns can break down trees, and your feet could crush rocks. Lions and tigers fear to approach you. Your strength and beauty are known to the whole world, and yet you walk about with a foolish monkey on your back. One blow of your horns would pierce him, and a stroke of your foot would crush him. Why do you not throw him to the ground and finish with this play?"

"This monkey is small," replied the buffalo, "and Nature has not given him much brain. Why then should I punish him? Moreover, why should I make him suffer in order that I may be happy?"

At this the fairy smiled, and with her magic wand she drove the monkey away. And she gave the great buffalo a charm by which no one could cause him to suffer again, and he then lived happy ever after.

13

The Sarabha

*He climbed the high walls with a strength greater than
that of the mightiest elephant*

here is a deer who lives so deep in a certain forest that no one ever sees him. Men call him the Sarabha. My little one, if you listen when all the world is quiet, and the sun is far away, you may hear his voice coming faintly from the woods.

One day a king was hunting in this forest, and he penetrated so far, so far, that one of these fair Sarabhas passed within his view.

"Who are you, beautiful creature?" he cried. But the Sarabha ran on and disappeared through the trees.

"I will catch him," exclaimed the King furiously; "he cannot escape me!" And darting forward upon his horse he shot arrows at the beautiful one. The arrows flew around the deer, but he feared them not, and ran over the grass as a bird flies through the air.

The King's horse raced faster and faster, and the forest, the hills, the valleys passed by unseen. His hunting-men, his army, his elephant-troops were left behind in the forest, searching in vain for their King. All were forgotten; nothing more on earth existed for the King; only the beautiful one he was pursuing.

"Run, run . . . faster . . . faster!" cried the King in fury. The hoofs of his horse hardly touched the ground as he galloped through space. But suddenly they reached a deep chasm, which the Sarabha had leaped easily across.

The King did not see the chasm; his eyes were set only on the quarry he was pursuing, but the horse perceived it and, not daring to jump, stopped suddenly at the edge, and the King was flung over his head deep into the chasm.

"Why do I no more hear the clatter of the horse's hoofs?" thought the Sarabha. "Has the King turned away, or has he perhaps fallen in the chasm?"

The Sarabha looked behind him and saw the horse running here and there riderless, and his heart was filled with sorrow.

"The King has fallen in the chasm! He is all alone! His army is far away! Surely he is suffering more than another would suffer in such a plight, for he has an army, glittering with gold, a hundred elephants, and men to guard him and await his call. But now he is alone, poor King! I will save him, if he be still alive."

Such were the thoughts of the Sarabha as he turned and went back to the chasm. On reaching the brink he looked down and saw his enemy lying in the dust, moaning. And, bending over, he spoke to him in a gentle voice: "King of men," he said, "do not fear me. I am not a goblin who does harm to those who are lost and far from home. I drink the water that you drink and eat the grass that grows on earth. I am able to help you, O King, and bring you out of this chasm. Trust me, I will come."

"Do my eyes see truly?" thought the King. "Is this not my enemy, who has come to help me?"

The King looked up at the Sarabha and his heart was full of shame.

"Fair one," he said, "I am not hurt over much, for the armor which covers me is strong. But the thought that I have been your enemy hurts me more than my wounds. Forgive me, blessed one."

Hearing these words, the Sarabha knew that the King trusted him and loved him. He descended into the chasm, and taking the King on his back, he climbed the high walls with a strength greater than that of the mightiest elephant, and brought him into the forest.

Then the King threw his arms around the Sarabha. "How can I thank you?" he said. "My palace, my country is yours. Come, dear one, return with me to the city. I cannot leave you here in the forest to be killed by hunters and wild animals."

"Great King," said the Sarabha, "do not ask me to go to your palace. Here is my country, in this forest; the trees are my palaces. But if you wish to make me happy, grant then this favor, I pray. Hunt no more in the forest, that those who live beneath the trees may be happy and free."

The King gave his promise gladly and returned to the palace, to the great joy of his people, who welcomed him with cheers. Then without more ado he published a decree that henceforth none should hunt in the forest again, wherefore the King and his people and the animals in the forest all lived happy ever after.

14

The Goblin Town

The others flew away to their homes on the back of the silver horse

great ship had been flung by the angry waves on the rocky shore of an island. Happily the crew and passengers, five hundred men in all, were not drowned. Their plight was wretched, however, but as they looked around they were cheered by their beautiful surroundings. "Our ship has sunk, alas!" they said, "but doubtless there are endless treasures in this island."

After awhile the sound of voices came to their ears and they saw a crowd of women approaching. Soon the women came to the place where the men were gathered and they spoke to them.

"Wherefrom do you come, O travelers?" they asked. "Has your ship been broken on the rocks? The men of this island left long ago in a ship, and have never returned. Come, then, with us to our homes, O travelers! We will care for you and make you happy."

Such were the alluring words of the women, but even as they spoke they bound the men with magic chains, and, not knowing they were drawn by these chains, the men followed the women to their homes. And so they lived some time in the city and ate the rice which the women prepared for them on golden dishes.

But one night, when all the men were asleep, one of the five hundred awoke and heard strange voices.

"Whose are those voices?" he thought. "Are they not the voices of goblins?"

He silently arose from his bed and hid behind a large stone to watch. He was soon rewarded, for he saw that the women, changed into goblins, were walking through the town.

"It is a goblin-town!" the man exclaimed in horror. "I must tell my companions. We must flee from here."

No sooner were his eyes thus opened than he saw that he was bound with chains.

When morning came he told his companions what he had seen. Some did not believe him, but the others asked, with trembling voices:

"How can we escape?"

"We cannot," the man replied. "With magic chains we are bound."

As he said these words, there was a flash of

light, and a white horse descended from the sky and landed before them.

And they heard a gentle voice from the sea which said:

"A flying horse, with silver wings, has answered to your call,
Mount on his back, your chains will break, and he will save you all."

And those who did not believe the story of their companion stayed with the women in the goblin-town, but the others flew away to their homes on the back of the silver horse and they all lived happy ever after.

~ 15 ~

The Great Elephant

*When the men reached the spot they gazed at the
giant-like form and a great fear seized them*

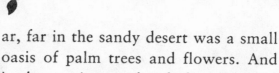

ar, far in the sandy desert was a small oasis of palm trees and flowers. And in that oasis, as a lonely hermit, lived an elephant, a beautiful elephant. He ate the fruit of the trees, and drank from a little stream of water that ran through the rocks. Happy he was, dancing through the banana trees, watching day and night come over the desert.

But one day, as he was dancing along, in the distance some strange voices came to his ears.

"Whose are those voices?" he said to himself. "Are they not voices of men, of unhappy men? Who are those men, and why do they cross the desert? Surely they are lost, or maybe they suffer some terrible pain."

Such were the thoughts of the handsome elephant as he walked in the direction of the voices. He walked some distance over the burning sand when he came upon a great crowd of men all huddled together at death's door, and at the piteous sight his eyes, for the first time in his happy life, filled with tears.

"O travelers," he said to them in a tender voice, "wherefrom do you come, and where are you going? Have you lost your way in the desert? Tell me, O men, that I may help you in some way."

So happy were the men to hear these friendly words that they fell on their knees before him.

"Beautiful one," they said, "we have been driven from our country by our King, and have roamed through the desert for many days. Not a drop of water have we found to drink, nor food to give us strength."

"Help us, O dear one," they cried; "help us."

"How many are you?" asked the elephant.

"We were one thousand," they replied, "but many have perished on the way."

The elephant gazed at them. One was crying for water, another asking for food.

"You are weak, O men," he said, "and the next city is too far for you to reach without food and drink. Therefore walk towards the hill which stands before you. At its foot you will find the body of a large elephant which will provide you with food, and nearby runs a stream of sweet water."

When he had thus spoken he ran over the

burning sand and disappeared as he had come.

"Where did the elephant go? And why did he run at such a pace?"

Straight to the hill he went, to the same hill he had pointed out to the men; but he took another way, that the men might not see him going. He climbed to the top of the hill and then from its highest point, in a mighty jump, his beautiful body crashed to the ground below.

When the men reached the spot they gazed at the giant-like form and a great fear seized them.

"Is this not our dear elephant?" exclaimed one among them.

"This face is the same face; the eyes, though closed, are the same eyes," said another.

And they all sat in the sand and wept bitterly.

After some time one among them spoke.

"Companions," he said, "we cannot eat this elephant who has give his life for us."

"Nay, friends," said another, "if we do not eat this elephant, his sacrifice will have been useless, and we shall die before reaching another city. Thus we shall not be helped, nor shall the wish of our elephant be fulfilled."

The men spoke no more but bent their heads in the burning sand and ate the meat with tears in their eyes. And it made them strong, very strong, so that they were able to cross the desert and reach a town where their troubles came to an end. They never forgot the great elephant, and they lived happy ever after.

～16～

The Quarrelsome Quails

Cry no more, my little ones. If you heed your King's
words you will never be caught

ark to those painful cries which pierce each day the silent forest! Alas! they are the cries of six thousand quails. Poor little birds! Each day a man comes from the village and casts a net over them as they land on the ground. After throwing the net, he pulls it together, catching hundreds of quails which he takes to the village to sell.

Now one day King Quail said: "Cry no more, my little ones. If you heed your King's words you will never be caught. When the net is thrown over you, put your heads through the holes, and all together fly up, lifting the net through the air. If then you land on the top of a thorny hill the prickles will hold the net above the ground and you can escape from under it before the villager reaches the hill. Do as I say, and you will all be saved. But if one day quarrels arise, and you should begin to fight one with another, alas! that day you will be caught and you will never see the woods again."

The quails did as their King advised, and when the net was thrown over them they flew up to a hill with it and escaped.

And the villager returned each day without a penny, and his wife was very, very angry.

"Do not worry," said he one evening to his wife. "Those naughty quails will fight together one of these days and then they will be easily caught."

And it happened one day that a quail stepped on the head of another.

"I will give you what you deserve!" cried the injured quail in anger, jumping at the other, and knocking his wing. "Away with you, away with you," he cried.

King Quail, seeing the quarrel, said to the others: "Let us not stay here. These two unhappy birds will surely come to a bad end." And he flew off with those who heeded his warning.

And while the two quarrelsome quails went on fighting, a strange dark cloud came over their heads. It was the net!

Many others were caught with them and taken to the village to be killed. But the wise King Quail, and those who heeded his counsel, were never caught. And in the silent little forest they all lived happy ever after.

~ 17 ~

The Forest Fire

The little one was not afraid; he gazed steadily at the flames

e good, my little ones," said Mother Quail to seven little quails, chirping in the nest. "Mother and Father will soon bring you little worms, and insects, and grass-seeds."

But each time Mother and Father Quail returned to the nest six little quails caught the worms and insects, but the seventh only ate the grass-seeds. And so while the wings of his brothers grew strong and firm, the little one's wings did not grow at all.

One night when the little family was tucked up cosily they were awakened by sad cries from the heart of the forest. Mother and Father Quail and the seven little quails peeped out of the nest.

What were those fiery red clouds hovering over the distant trees?

The little quails began to cry, and Mother and Father held them tight within their wings.

Crackle . . . crackle . . . bzz . . . bzz . . . roared the large red clouds.

"See, Father," exclaimed the seventh little one, "it is a fire in the woods."

The glowing flames advanced with the speed of wind through the forest, burning every bush and tree in their path. The roar came nearer and nearer, and soon the fire approached the nest. There was no time to lose and, dashing forth, Mother and Father Quail and the six little quails flew away. But the seventh little one remained alone, he had no wings to fly with.

Bzz . . . bzz . . . roared the large red clouds as they danced around the nest. But the little one was not afraid; he gazed steadily at the flames with his two small twinkling eyes, and in his soft chirping voice he spoke to them.

"I am small," he said, "and have no wings. Why do you come to this wee nest where I am left alone? Go your way, mighty flames; there is nothing here for you."

As he spoke the raging fire slunk away and disappeared through the trees, and the forest became silent as after a storm.

By and by little voices arose from the moss, and the frogs signaled that all was clear. One by one little heads peeped out of their hiding places. The smoke clouds had blown far away and Queen Moon smiled once more through the trees. Little Quail also smiled in his nest as he saw the forest waking up again, and he lived there happy ever after.

18

The End
of the World

He reached a certain mountain which lay in their path

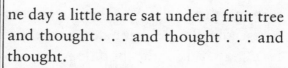

One day a little hare sat under a fruit tree and thought . . . and thought . . . and thought.

What, my children, did the little hare think about under the tree?

"What will happen to me when the earth comes to an end?" he thought, and at that very moment a fruit fell from the tree. Off ran little hare as fast as his legs could carry him, so sure he was that the noise of the fruit falling to the ground was that of the earth breaking to pieces. And he ran and ran, not daring to look behind him.

"Brother, brother," called another little hare who saw him running, "pray tell me what has happened!"

But the little hare ran on and did not even turn to answer. But the other hare ran after him, calling louder and louder: "What has happened, little brother, what has happened?"

At last little hare stopped a moment and said: "The earth is breaking to pieces!" At this the other hare started running still faster and a third hare joined them, and a fourth, and a fifth, till a hundred thousand hares were racing through the fields. And they raced through the forest and the deep jungles, and the deer, the boars, the elks, the buffaloes, the oxen, the rhinoceros, the tigers, the lions, and the elephants, hearing that the earth was coming to an end, all ran wildly with them.

But among those living in the jungle was a lion, a wise lion, who knew everything that took place in the world. And when it became known to him that so many hundreds and thousands of animals were running away because they believed that the earth was breaking to pieces, he thought: "This earth of ours is far from coming to an end, but my poor creatures will die if I do not save them, for in their fright they will run into the sea." And he ran at such a pace that he reached a certain mountain which lay in their path before they came to it. And as they passed by the mountain he roared three times with such a mighty roar that they stopped in their mad flight and stood still close to each other, trembling.

The great lion descended from the mountain and approached them. "Why are you running at such a pace?" he asked.

"The earth is breaking to pieces," they replied.

"Who saw it breaking to pieces?" he asked.

"The elephants," they replied.

"Did you see it breaking?" he asked the elephants.

"No, we did not see it; the lions saw it," they replied.

"Did you see it?" he asked the lions.

"No, the tigers saw it," they replied.

"Did you see it?" he asked the tigers.

"The rhinoceros saw it," they replied.

But the rhinoceros said: "The oxen saw it." The oxen said: "The buffaloes saw it." The buffaloes said: "The elks saw it." The elks said: "The boars saw it." The boars said: "The deer saw it." The deer said: "The hares saw it." And the hares said: "That little one told us that the earth was breaking."

"Did you see the earth breaking?" he asked little hare.

"Yes, lord," replied the hare, "I saw it breaking."

"Where were you when you saw it breaking?" he asked.

With a trembling voice little hare replied: "I was sitting beneath a fruit tree and I thought: 'What will happen to me when the earth comes to an end?' And at the very moment I heard the noise of the earth breaking, and I ran."

The great lion thought: "He was sitting beneath a fruit tree; certainly the noise he heard was that of a fruit falling to the ground."

"Ride on my back, little one," he said, "and show me where you saw the earth break."

Little hare jumped on his back and the great lion flew to the place, but as they approached the fruit tree little hare jumped off, so frightened he was to return to the spot. And he pointed out the tree to the lion, saying: "Lord, there is the tree."

The great one went to the tree and saw the spot where little hare had been sitting and the fruit which had fallen from the tree. "Come here, little one," he called. "Now where do you see the earth broken?"

Little hare, after looking around, and seeing the fruit on the ground, knew that there had been no occasion for his fright; he jumped once again on the lion's back and away they went to the hundreds and thousands of creatures who were awaiting their return.

The lion then told the great multitude that the noise little hare had heard was of a fruit falling to the ground.

And so all turned back, the elephants to the jungle, the lions to the caves, the deer to the river banks, and little hare to the fruit tree, and they all lived happy ever after.

~19~

The Golden Goose

*When the great red sun appeared in the sky, and the two
small geese spread their wings, he followed them*

"olden clouds are passing over our city!"
one day shouted the people of Benares,
for the sky was covered with gold. It
was neither a cloud nor the gold that
a star may leave on its way; the gold was
flowing from the wings of a goose, a beautiful
goose, flying slowly and majestically through
the air.

The King looked up from the tower of his
palace. "Great bird," he exclaimed in amazement, "of those who fly through space you are
certainly the king."

And he called his courtiers; music was
played, garlands of flowers and perfumes were
brought, and thus the King honored the beautiful visitor.

The goose looked down, and seeing the King
and his courtiers, and the garlands of flowers,
and hearing the sweet music, he turned to the
flock of geese that followed him:

"Why does the King honor me in this way?"
he asked.

"Lord, surely he wishes to be your friend,"
replied the geese.

At this the golden bird descended to the earth

and greeted the King; he then returned to his companions in the sky.

On the following day the King was walking through the gardens near the lake of Anokkatta when the great bird came again to him, carrying water on one wing, and powder of sandalwood on the other. His visit was no longer than before, for after sprinkling the water upon the King, and dusting the powder over him, he immediately rejoined his companions and flew away to his kingdom at Cittakutta.

As time passed the King of Benares longed more and more to see the golden bird again. Every day he walked near the lake Anokkatta, and every day, looking into the far horizon, he sighed: "Will my friend return once again?"

But the golden one was far away, in the mountains at Cittakutta, with his flock of ninety thousand geese. All loved their King and were very, very happy.

But one day the two youngest of the flock went to the King, and after bowing very low, they said:

"We come to take leave of you, O King! We are going to run a race with the sun."

"My little ones," the King replied, "your

small wings are too weak to fly with the sun;
you would perish on the way; therefore be wise
and do not go."

But the young geese persisted. They asked a
second time, and a third time, when, hearing
none but the same answer from their King,
they decided to leave without his permission.

So before sunrise they stole away to Mount
Yughandara and waited till the sun appeared.

But the King knew that the foolish little geese
had left, and that they stood waiting on
Yughandara. He flew swiftly to the mountain
and when the great red sun appeared in the
sky, and the two small geese spread their wings,
he followed them.

When the smallest one had flown for a few
hours his wings beat feebly and they could
carry him no farther. But the King was flying
at his side, and when he saw that the young
one was about to fall to the ground he went
up to him, and soothed him, and bore him on
his wings to Cittakutta.

Then the golden one flew back to the other
little goose, and, flying faster than the sun, he
reached him and flew at his side.

"Lord," cried the young goose, "I can fly no

longer." The great bird took him gently on his wing and him too he bore to Cittakutta.

"What if I should outrace the sun, which stands just now at its zenith?" thought the great bird.

And piercing the clouds, piercing the space, he overran the sun a thousand times.

But after a while he thought: "What is the sun to me? Why should I race with him? A far greater mission awaits me. I will go to my friend the King of Benares and speak wisely to him, and he and his people will be happy."

He then flew over the whole world, from one end to the other, till at last he reached Benares.

Once again the city was illumined with a golden haze. And descending slowly, the golden one alighted before a window of the palace.

"My friend has come!" cried the King joyfully. And cheers resounded through the palace. The King himself brought a golden throne for the bird, and bade him: "Come in and sit with me."

And after refreshing his wings with perfume and giving him sweet water to drink, the King

sat at his side that they might converse together.

"Wherefrom do you come, O beautiful bird?
Ever since you flew over Benares, I have longed
to see you again," said the King.

"I come from Cittakutta, from the silent
mountains," the great goose replied.

He then told the King the story of his race
with the sun. The eyes of the King glistened as
he listened.

"Is it possible that I may see you race with
the sun?" he humbly asked the bird.

"Nay," replied the goose, "that can never
be seen. But it is possible that I may show you
in another way, O King, the speed of my
flight."

"In what way, beautiful bird?" asked the
King.

"Call forth four archers," said the bird, "and
order them to shoot their arrows into a wall,
all at once, and before they touch the wall I
will catch them in my beak."

The King did as the bird asked, and as the
four archers shot their arrows, the great one
caught them. Not one arrow touched the wall.

"Marvelous!" exclaimed the King. "Can any speed be compared to yours, O miraculous one?"

"Yes," replied the bird, "there is a speed greater than mine. A hundred times faster, a thousand times, a hundred thousand times faster is the speed of Time. Pleasures, riches, palaces! Time takes them away faster than my fastest flight."

The King hearing these words trembled with fright. But the bird consoled him and spoke to him gently:

"O King," he said, "fear not. If you love your people and try to make them happy, what matters it if time goes on?"

Tears filled the eyes of the King. "Great one," he said, "leave me not alone to rule. Stay always at my side in the palace and speak to me, that I may be happy, and make my people happy."

"Nay," said the golden one, "I will not remain. One day, after drinking wine, you might say: 'Kill that bird, that we may feast on him.'"

"Never would I taste of wine while you are here!" exclaimed the King.

"The cries of lions and birds are clear and true," said the goose, "but the words of men are not as true as these. Nay, I will return to my kingdom and if you love me we shall be friends, though far away."

"Shall I never see you again?" exclaimed the King.

"One day perhaps I shall return," said the goose, "and then we shall see each other again."

With these words he unfolded his wings and soared into the air; the sky became golden again and the kingdom was happy ever after.

20

The Noble Horse

*On returning to the palace the noble creature sank
to the ground*

y little ones, how you would have loved to stroke the silky neck of so fair a creature as the beloved horse of Brahmadatta, King of Benares.

More beautiful, more handsome than any other horse in the world he was, swift as a deer and graceful as a swan. There was a tender light in his eyes and his steps were so majestic that he could not have been other than a king.

His stable was a palace. A lamp with perfumed oil burned in it day and night, and soft rose curtains with stars of gold hung above his head.

At that time Benares was the happiest kingdom in India. It was rich and flourishing, and far grander than any other state. Therefore many other kings were envious and some of them resolved to fight against it, fearing that it would become more powerful than they.

Seven of these kings gathered their armies and marched towards the mighty state, and Brahmadatta called one of his knights.

"Our enemies," he said, "are approaching the gates of the city; your King and your country are in danger. Can you, my brave warrior, fight against seven kings?"

"Not only against seven kings," the knight replied, "but against a hundred kings, lord, if I may ride your horse, your noble one."

"Take my horse," replied Brahmadatta, "and fly to the battle. Return to us victorious; your King and your country trust you."

Thus the knight, mounted on the gallant horse, dashed to the battle, and as a storm passing over a field of wheat he laid the first enemy low, captured the King, and brought him prisoner to Benares.

Again he rushed to the battlefield, defeated the second army, and took the second King prisoner.

A similar fate befell the third, fourth, and fifth Kings, but in capturing the sixth the knight's horse was wounded.

On returning to the palace the noble creature sank to the ground and the knight tenderly removed its harness. But he might not stay, and so another horse was brought.

As the knight was about to mount his new steed the wounded horse opened his eyes, and he thought: "My brave rider will be killed; on another horse he could never prevail against the seventh army. Benares will be taken by the enemy."

And, calling the knight, he spoke to him in a deep voice.

"Brave knight," he said, "be wise. Do not take another horse, for I alone can enable you to defeat the seventh army. Put my armor on my back once more, and together we will gain the victory."

The knight bound up the noble creature's wounds, mounted on his back, and rode away to the battlefield. The foe were many and the fight was hard, but at last the seventh army was defeated, and the seventh King captured.

But when the battle was over the noble horse fell bleeding to the ground.

The King knelt at his side and caressed him, and a soft whisper came from his lips.

"Be not sad, my King," he said; "my wounds do not pain me, for the victory is won. But do not slay those who are now your prisoners. Let them return to their homes promising never to attack Benares again."

Then, having spoken these words, the great one closed his eyes and died.

But his memory lived long in the land and Brahmadatta heeded his counsel.

The seven kings were released, and war never again broke out. The people of all the kingdoms loved each other, and they all lived happy ever after.

Other books of myth and legend from Inner Traditions

Peronnik

A French Fairy Tale of the Grail Quest

Emile Souvestre • Illustrated by Christiane Lesch
ISBN 0-89281-061-0 • $9.95 cloth
Full-color illustrations

With rich symbolism and evocative illustrations, *Peronnik* recalls the timeless myth of Parsival and the Grail. In this charming story, Peronnik, a cheerful young wanderer, learns of a magical life-giving chalice and a powerful dimaond lance which are in the possession of a giant sorcerer. Many brave knights have sought these treasures, but none have returned from the enchanted forest. Peronnik chooses to pursue the quest, armed only with his wits and purity of heart. In the dangers and trials he faces along the way, we are able to rejoice in his courage and resourcefulness, and applaud his essential virtues.

Emile Souvestre was born in 1806 in Brittany, France, and was a well-known collector and teller of folk tales from his native region. *Peronnik* is one of his most famous stories, and was part of a collection of Breton folk tales first published in 1845.

Kalila and Dimna

Tales for Kings and Commoners

Retold by Ramsay Wood

ISBN 0-89281-061-0 • $12.95 paperback

The eternal *Fables of Bidpai* originated nearly 2,000 years ago in a Sanskrit collection of animal tales called the *Panchatantra*. These delightful and humorous stories have found their way into the folklore of every major culture and tradition, influencing and inspiring such classics as *Aesop's Fables*, *The Arabian Nights*, *The Canterbury Tales*, and even *Uncle Remus*.

Instructive and entertaining, these stories within stories are ostensibly a handbook for rulers. But in their slyly profound grasp of human nature at its best—and more often, at its worst—they are clearly meant as good counsel for us all.

"This is a beautiful book full of mirth, human interest, unsentimental wisdom, and vigorous writing."

—**Boston Globe**

"These are wise and vigorous, sly and funny tales...They are contemporary: they are eternal...no higher praise is necessary."

—**Carlos Fuentes**

Masters of Enchantment
The Lives and Legends of the Mahasiddhas
Keith Dowman • Illustrated by Robert Beer
ISBN 0-89281-061-0 • $12.95 paperback
ISBN 0-89281-053-X • $29.95 clothbound
32 full-color illustrations• Line art throughout

This beautifully illustrated collection of stories, skillfully retold from the original twelfth century A.D. text, tells the legends of the saints and magicians who founded the lineages of the Tantric Buddhist tradition. Extraordinary men and women from all walks of life, the Mahasiddhas demonstrate that enlightenment may be found in the most unexpected circumstances.

"The book is an inspired creation—the collaboration of Dowman, an eminent translator/interpreter of Tibetan Buddhism, and Beer, a master thangka painter and artistic visionary, has produced a book of high merit and high adventures, stories through whose cosmic transparency shines the illimitable Buddha-nature."

—Small Press Review

"We are drawn into the Mahasiddhas' magnificent magical vision of the universe, and we can take innocent delight in their often quirky personalities, their tremendous sense of humor, and their penchant for miraculous feats. This volume is an exemplary achievement and should be in the hands of every student of spirituality." **—Spectrum Review**

These and other Inner Traditions titles are available at many fine bookstores or, to order directly from the publisher, send a check or money order for the total amount, payable to Inner Traditions, plus $2.00 shipping and handling for the first book and $1.00 for each additional book to:

Inner Traditions
One Park Street
Rochester, VT 05767

Be sure to request a free catalog.